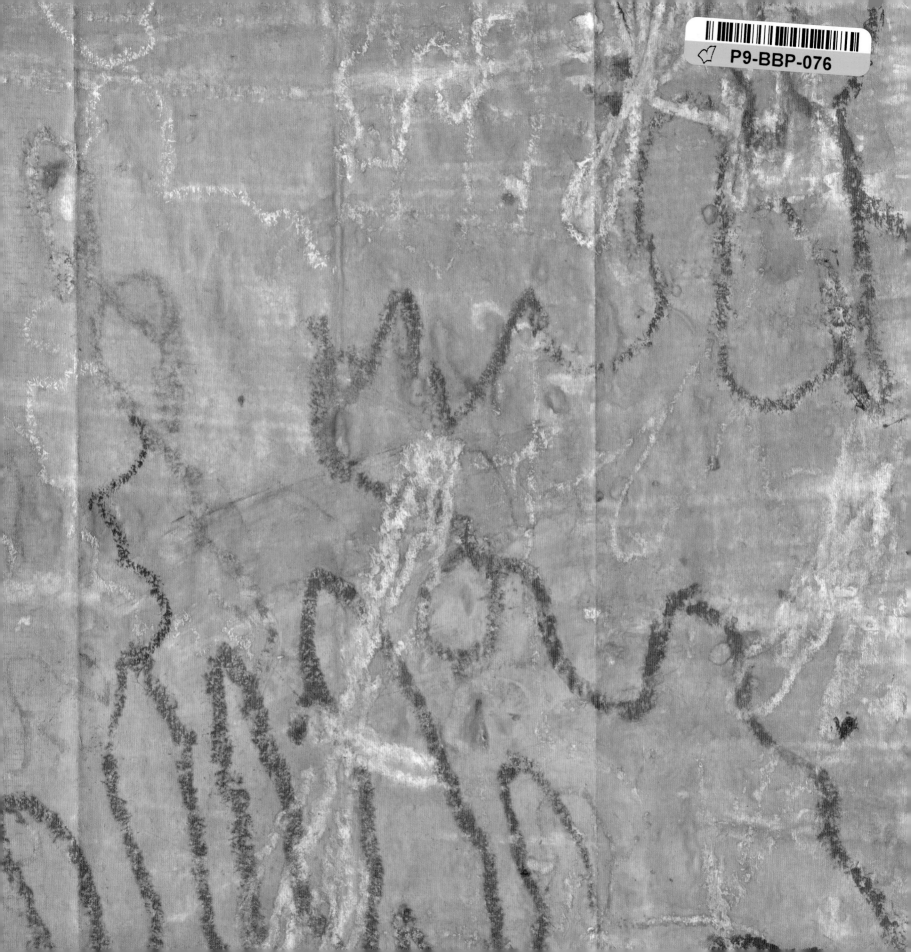

POETREES

Douglas Florian

Beach Lane Books
New York London Toronto Sydney

Of blessed memory of my aunt
Betty Ginsberg, a lover of books

CONTENTS

BEACH LANE BOOKS
An imprint of Simon & Schuster Children's Publishing Division
1230 Avenue of the Americas, New York, New York 10020
Copyright © 2010 by Douglas Florian
All rights reserved, including the right of reproduction in whole or in part in any form.
BEACH LANE BOOKS is a trademark of Simon & Schuster, Inc.
For information about special discounts for bulk purchases, please contact Simon &
Schuster Special Sales at 1-866-506-1949 or business@simonandschuster.com.
The Simon & Schuster Speakers Bureau can bring authors to your live event. For
more information or to book an event, contact the Simon & Schuster Speakers
Bureau at 1-866-248-3049 or visit our website at www.simonspeakers.com.
The text for this book is set in Sabon LT.
The illustrations for this book are rendered in gouache watercolor paints, colored
pencils, rubber stamps, oil pastels, and collage on primed brown paper bags.
Manufactured in China * 1109 SCP
First Edition
2 4 6 8 10 9 7 5 3 1
Library of Congress Cataloging-in-Publication Data
Florian, Douglas.
Poetrees / Douglas Florian.—1st ed.
p. cm.
ISBN 978-1-4169-8672-0 (alk. paper)
1. Trees—Juvenile poetry. 2. Children's poetry, American. I. Title.
PS3556.L589P64 2010
811'.54—dc22   2009003025

The Seed

Inside this seed you'll find a stem and leaf that grow with rain into a trunk and branch and leaf and seed that starts again.

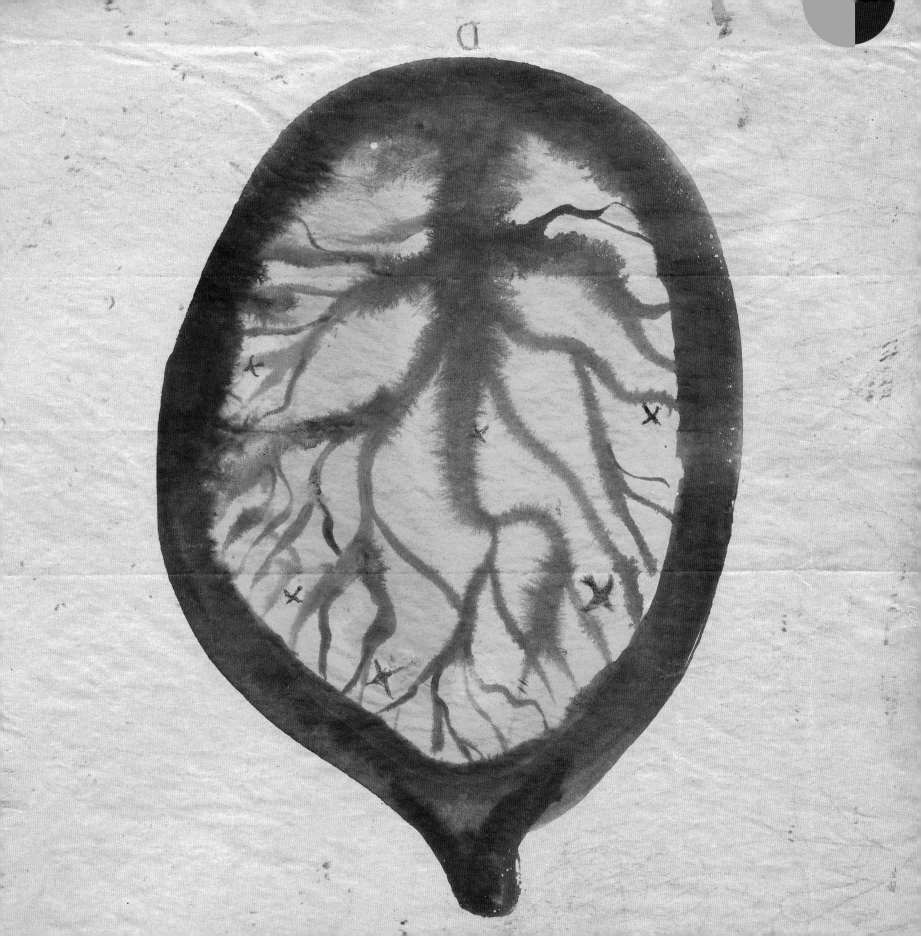

Oak

From the acorn
Grows the tree—

S l o w l y ,

S l o w l y .

Coconut Palm

I'm nuts about the coconut.
I'm cuckoo for the coco.
I'm crazed for this amazing nut.
For coco I am loco.
I'm never calm to climb this palm.
I scurry up and hurry
To knock one down onto the ground,
Then eat it in a flurry.

Jug tree.
Hug tree.
Upside-
Down tree.
Vat tree.
Fat tree.
Bottle tree.
Brown tree.
Double tree.
Bubble tree.
Can-dle-stick.
G i r t h tree.
E a r t h tree.
T h i c k !
T h i c k !
T h i c k !

Roots

The roots of trees
Don't just grow d
         o
           w
            n.

They b r a n c h out
Sideways, underground,
To help the tree to get a grip,
To anchor it so it won't slip.
As root hairs drink
The rain that p
           o
           u
           r
           s

They sip it up like tiny straws.
While by the growing roots in holes
Live badgers, rabbits, moles, and voles.
They tunnel under roots of trees
And *root* there for their families.

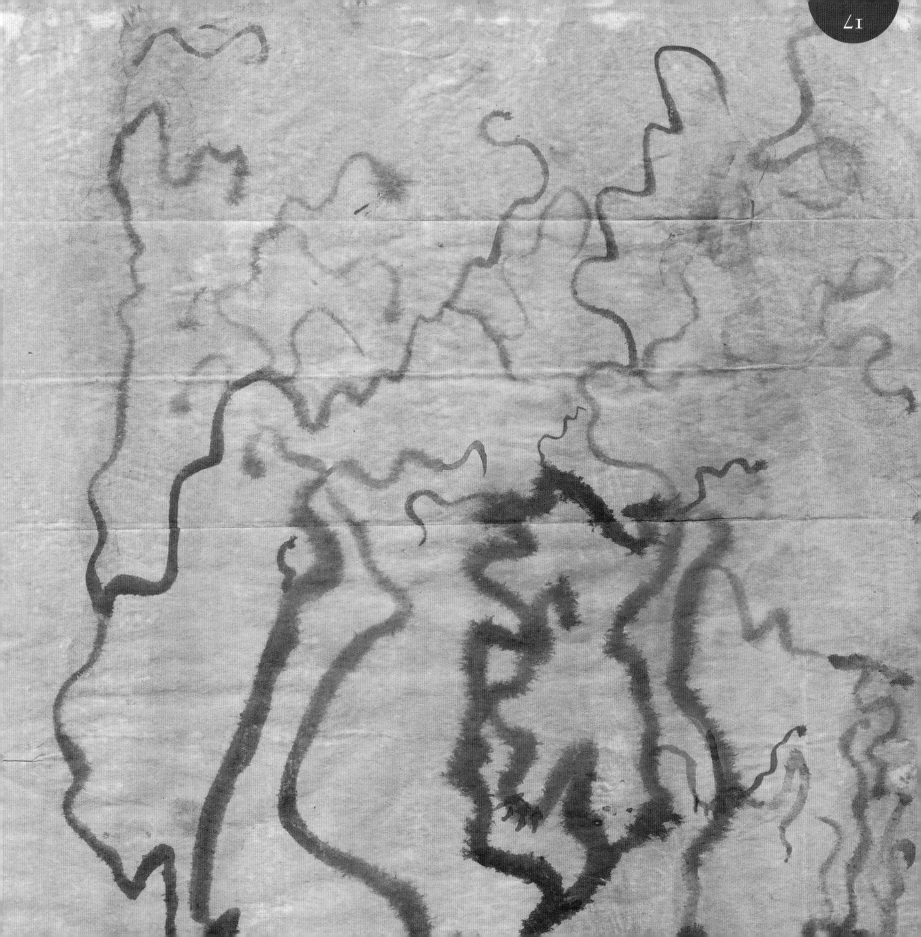

Giant Sequoias

Ancient seers
Of three thousand years.
Heavenly high.
Friends to the sky.
Spongy thick bark.
Large as an ark.
Gargantuan girth.
Anchored in earth.
Grow by degrees
To world's tallest trees.
Never destroy a
Giant sequoia.

Scribbly Gum

The scribbly gum's smooth gray bark
Has lines where larvae left their mark.
Their nibbling left a scribbly drawing—
A work of art by boring, gnawing.
From their munching, lunching, chewing—
Lovely *woodcuts* for the viewing.

Banyan

A fig tree.
A big tree.
An acre in its canopy.
A s p r e a d i n g tree.
A treading tree.
An always-outward-heading tree.
One hundred trunks grow side by side.
One thousand pillar roots spread wide.
Branches,

          trunks,

               and roots in chorus.

It's not a tree—
It's a **forest!**

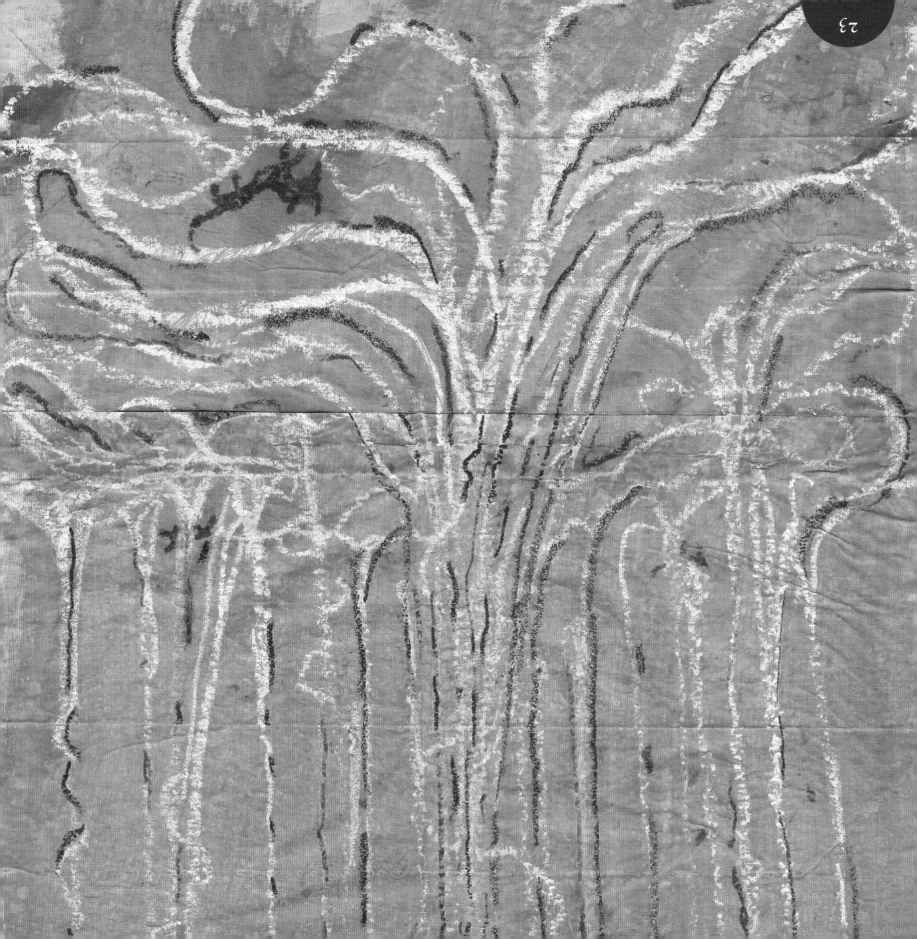

Monkey Puzzle Tree

It's said that a monkey could climb
Up this tree in the quickest of time.
　　But climbing back down
　　Without cracking its crown
Is a puzzle so hard, it's a crime.

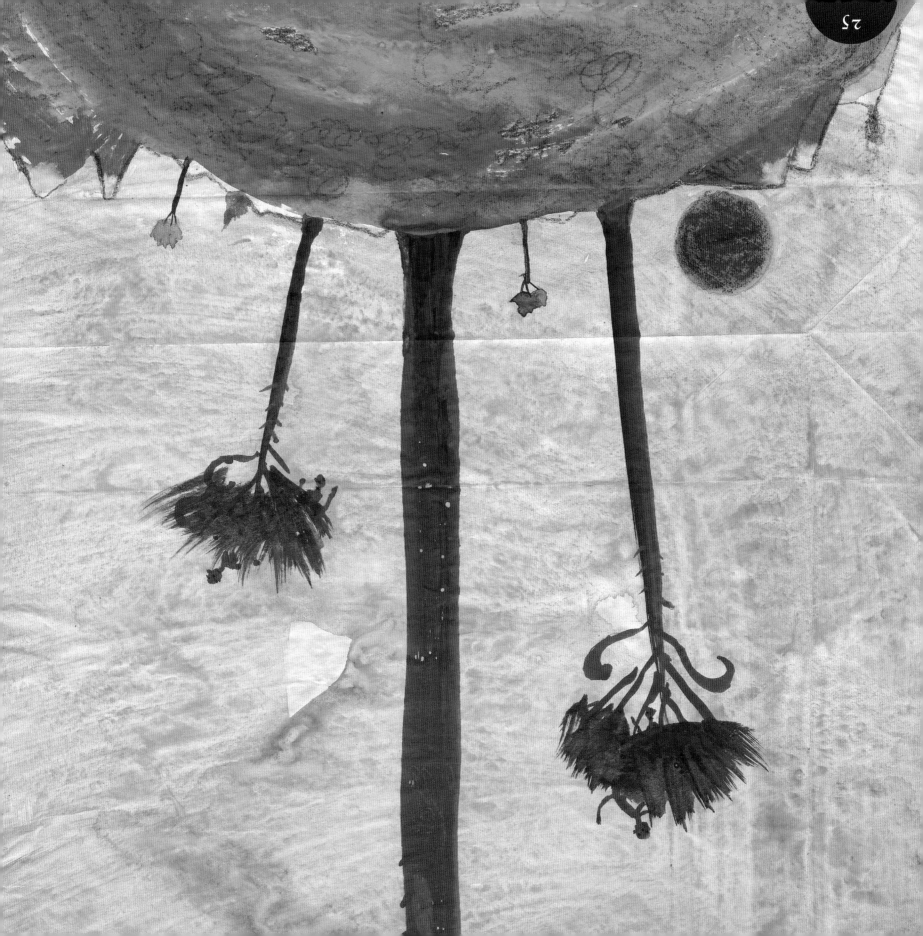

Paper Birch

Paper birch.
White birch.
Canoe birch too.
Beautiful
Native
Tree to view.
Smooth white birch bark
Grows where it's cold.
Paper birrrrrrrrrrrrch:
A sight to behold.

Tree Rings

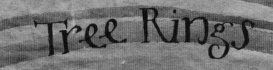

Tree rings show
how trees grow.

Wide rings: fast growth.

Narrow rings: slow.

Heartwood: dead wood.

Sapwood: living.

A tree's true his-tree

free for the giving.

Bristlecone Pine

I am no ordinary tree—
I'm master of longevity.
One of the oldest trees on Earth,
With swirling branches, twirling girth.
And where it's cold and dry I thrive:
For fifty cen-trees I'm alive.
I cope on slopes ten thousand feet high.
I'm Bristlecone Pine—
I never say die!

Leaves

Lobed leaves.
Oval leaves.
Smooth leaves or jagged.
Heart-shaped.
Odd-shaped.
Leaves eaten ragged.
Fan-like.
Hand-like.
Light leaves.
Dark.
Leathery.
Feathery.
Leaves in a park.
Two points.
Ten points.
Points like a saw.
Lovely leaves
Leave me in awe.

33

Bark

The outer bark of trees is dead,
So when trees grow, the bark is shed.
It cracks.
        It flakes.
               It splits.
                    It peels.
From fire, heat, and cold it shields.
It comes in an array of hues—
Of browns or reds or greens or blues.
It's rough or tough
Or strewn with spines.
Bumpy, lumpy, filled with lines.
Or found with fronds
That all jut out.
The bark's a thing to **bark** about.

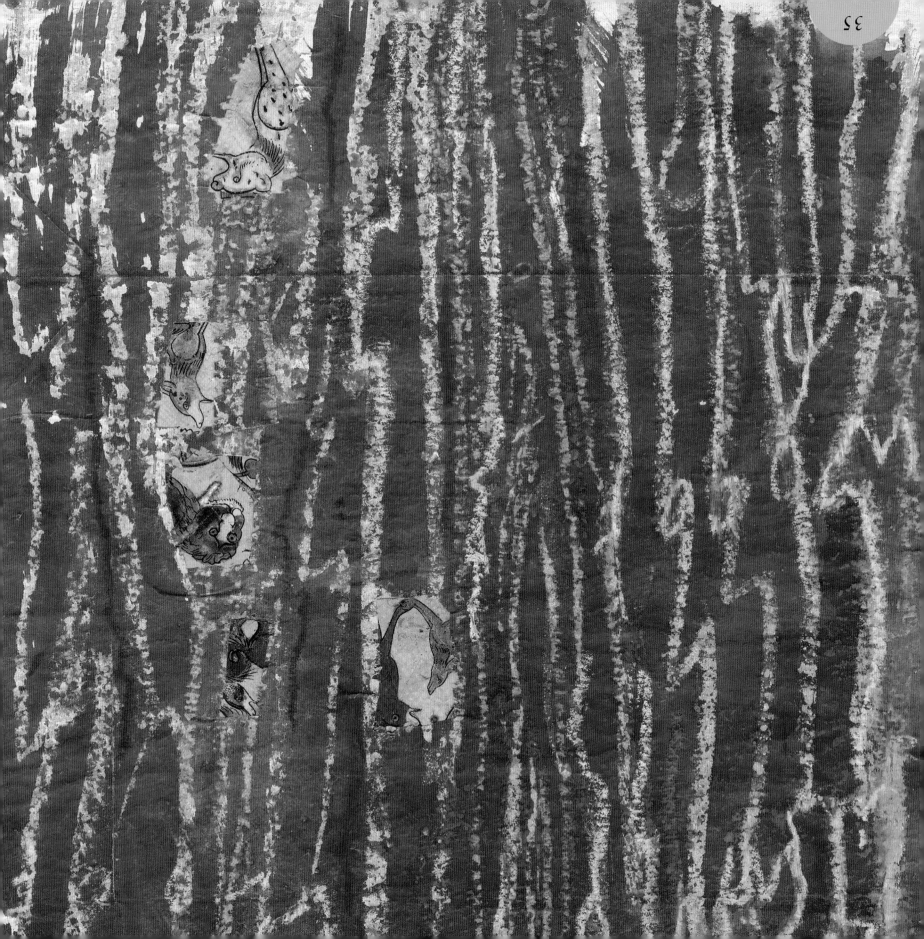

Dragon Tree

The dragons all heap scorn on me
Because I'm born an earthly tree.
While dragons roam and dragons race,
I'm stuck at home, tied to one place.
For though my sap is dragon's blood,
My roots are trapped in dirt and mud.
Great claws I grow,
But I can't gore.
And I don't know
To even roar.
In dragon dreams I scheme to fly
And scream in fire across the sky
To leave this lowly life *terrestrial*,
And soar, what's more, in skies *celestial*.

Japanese Cedar

Japanese cedar:
Ex-seed-ingly fine.
Tree-mendous.
Stupendous.
For some it's divine.
Ex-seed-ingly old.
Ex-seed-ingly tall.
And all from a seed so
Ex-seed-ingly small.

Weeping Willow

Willow tree, why do you weep?
Why do you cry and moan?

All day these caterpillars creep.
They won't let me alone!

Willow tree, why do you bend
Your branches to the ground?

I bend my branches low to send
Those caterpillars down!

Yews

Yew may find yews near a grave—
Huge trunks hollow as a cave,
Home to gnomes and elves and trolls,
Sneaking peeks at yew through holes.
Inside yew may view a chair.
Or a maple table there.
Yews are spooky; gloomy, too.
Yew've got one behind yew—
Boo!

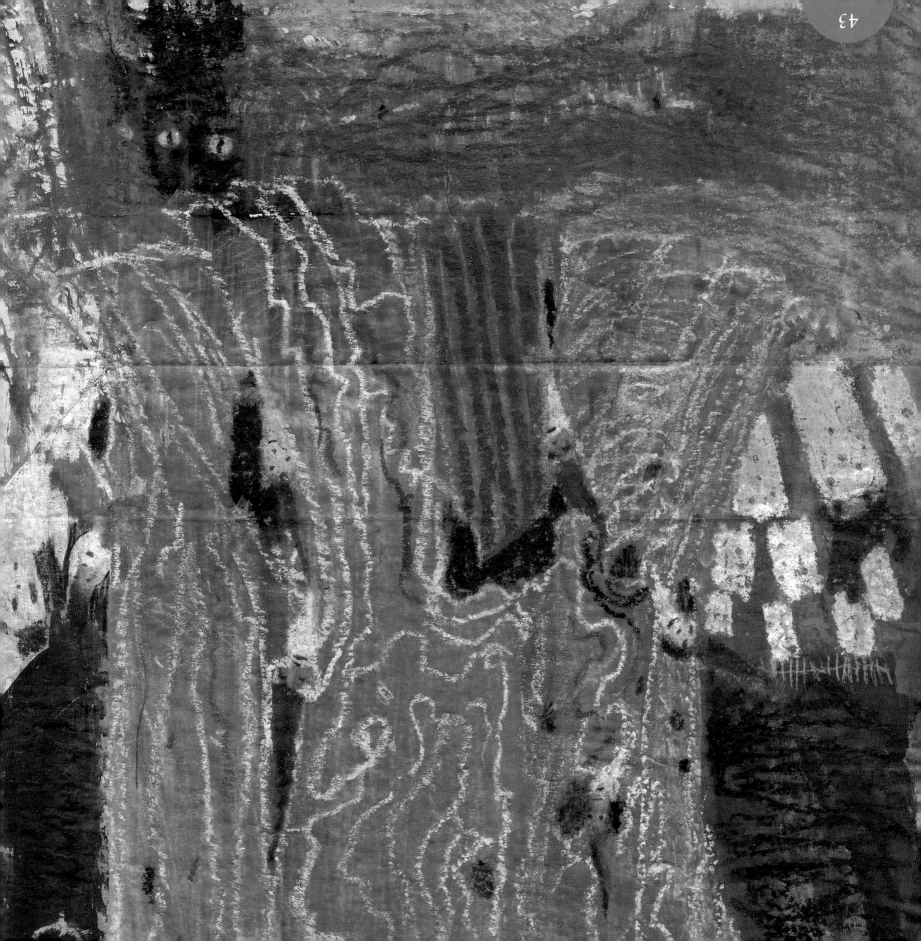

Glossatree

Banyan

The banyan is a fig tree from India, where it is the national tree. Merchants there called *banias* would trade under its shade. Older banyan trees drop hundreds of roots from their branches. These "prop roots" eventually grow into trunks and help the tree spread out widely. In the Hindu religion the banyan tree is considered sacred.

Baobab

There are eight species of baobab, six of them native to Madagascar. Thousands of baobabs grow in Australia, where the Aboriginal people believe that they are sacred and hold the spirits of their ancestors. In Africa during a drought, elephants may open the trunk of this tree to chew on the moist wood inside. The unusual shapes of baobabs resemble objects such as bottles, teapots, and candlesticks. The baobab is sometimes called an upside-down tree because its sparse branches look like roots.

Bark

The outer skin of a tree is called the bark. It keeps the tree from drying out and protects it from attacks by animals, parasites, and diseases. Bark has two layers. The inner layer, called cambium, has living cells still growing. The outer layer has dead cells that act as a barrier.

Bristlecone Pine

Bristlecone pines are among the oldest living things on Earth. Some specimens are nearly 5,000 years of age. The oldest bristlecone pine is called Methuselah, after the longest-living character in the Bible. This tree can be found in the harsh, windswept habitat of the Ancient Bristlecone Pine Forest, which is located in the White Mountains of California.

Coconut Palm

This tree is found throughout the tropics, as it requires a warm, humid climate with lots of sun. It can grow to a height of about 100 feet. The tasty coconut is the fruit of the coconut palm. This species may have originated somewhere around the Indian Ocean. The most ancient known fossil of a coconut-like plant is more than 15 million years old and was found in Bangladesh.

Paper Birch

The paper birch got its name because people once used its white bark as a writing scroll. This tree is also known as the white birch because of its white bark and the canoe birch because Native Americans used its waterproof bark as a covering for canoes. The paper birch is most common in the cold climates of North America.

Roots

The roots of trees don't only grow downward; they also grow outward, usually to a much greater degree. At the tips of roots are fine root hairs that absorb water and minerals from the soil. Burrowing animals such as badgers live among the roots of trees.

Scribbly Gum

This medium-sized eucalyptus tree is found in the plains and hills near Sydney, Australia. The scribbly lines on its bark are made by the larvae of the scribbly gum moth that burrow and live between layers of the bark.

Seeds

A seed is a baby plant (embryo) encased in a covering called a seed coat. Seeds grow from two places: the stem and the root. Orchid seeds are the world's smallest, with a million seeds weighing only a gram. The seed from the coco de mer palm is the world's largest, weighing up to 65 pounds. Some primitive plants like mosses or ferns don't have seeds and must reproduce using other means.

Tree Rings

Also called annual rings and growth rings, the rings that appear in a slice of tree trunk show the tree's age and growth patterns. Narrow rings indicate slow growth, while wide rings indicate fast growth. The fastest growth usually occurs during the rainy spring season. The tree's heartwood, which is closer to the center of the tree and often appears darker, is made mostly of dead cells. The surrounding lighter sapwood is still living.

Weeping Willow

The weeping willow, named for its drooping branches, is native to China. It grows best in moist soil, often near ponds and lakes. It may reach a height of about 45 feet. Many species of caterpillars feed on the long leaves of this tree.

Dragon Tree

There are about 60 different species of dragon trees, most of which are native to Africa. All have branches that look like the claws of a dragon and deep red sap that has reminded people of blood. The oldest dragon tree is thought to be more than 600 years of age.

Giant Sequoia

The giant sequoia is one of the world's biggest and oldest tree species. The largest one, named General Sherman, lives in California's Sequoia National Park. This tree is more than 270 feet tall and has a trunk that's 30 feet in diameter. Giant sequoias became rare after many were harvested for lumber. These trees are native to the western side of the Sierra Nevada mountain range in California.

Japanese Cedar

This large evergreen is called *Sugi* in Japan, where it grows wild and can reach a height of 200 feet and a girth of 50 feet. It is considered sacred and is often planted near temples. Despite being called a cedar, this tree is actually a member of the cypress family. The oldest known Japanese cedar, called *Jomon Sugi*, may be more than 2,000 years of age.

Leaves

Leaves are like little power stations for the tree. They take the energy from sunlight to turn carbon dioxide and water into sugars. These sugars can be used as fuel for the tree or to make tree cells (cellulose). This process is called photosynthesis. Leaves also store water and food for the tree. They come in a variety of shapes and sizes. Leaves are usually green because they contain a compound called chlorophyll that helps in photosynthesis.

Monkey Puzzle Tree

Originally from the Andes Mountains of Chile and Argentina, this tree was first grown in England around 1850. It was there that, upon seeing the trees' spiky leaf points, someone said, "It would puzzle a monkey to climb that." Of course there aren't any monkeys living in this tree's native Andean habitat, where it is called *Pehuén*. This species is very old, and the spiky leaves likely evolved to discourage dinosaurs from eating them.

Oak

There are approximately 600 species of oak. This hardwood tree grows slowly from an acorn, a hard-shelled seed with a pointed tip on top and scaly cup beneath. Oak lumber is used in many things, including furniture, flooring, and barrels.

Yew

The yew is common in England, where it once was used to make bows and arrows. This tree is often found near the churchyards and graveyards of England, Scotland, and Ireland. The humid climates of these countries can cause the yews' trunks to decay until they become completely hollow. People have been known to fit the hollow trunks with tables and chairs. The Fortingall Yew in Scotland is believed to be more than 3,000 years old.

Author's Note

I grew up in a neighborhood in Queens, New York, that was filled with young sycamore trees. In the summer, when my mother wasn't looking, my friend and I would climb these trees and enjoy the view from high above. In the autumn we would break open the hard brown spheres of the trees' fruit and watch the seeds scatter in the wind. Sometimes we would also peel away the rough brown bark of the trunk to see the smooth green and yellow bark—and the occasional insect—hidden beneath. There were also many maples, weeping willows, pin oaks, honey locusts, pines, and a few magnificent elms in this green oasis in New York City. Over the years those trees have grown taller and wider in girth, just as I have. And although I no longer climb trees, I do still love to draw them, paint them, study them, write poems about them, and enjoy their beauty and shade with my children.

Trees are an essential part of our planet. By absorbing carbon dioxide, they help reduce global warming. They protect our soil from erosion. And they provide necessities such as lumber, paper, fruit, and nuts. This is why it's so important for us to conserve and preserve our trees—along with all the other plants, animals, and habitats that call Earth home.

While creating this book, I relied on the following texts:

LITTLE, ELBERT, L. *National Audubon Society Field Guide to North American Trees: Eastern Region.* New York: Knopf, 1980.

———. *National Audubon Society Field Guide to North American Trees: Western Region.* New York: Knopf, 1980.

MARINELLI, JANET, ed. *Plant.* New York: DK Publishing, 2005. First published in 2004 by Dorling Kindersley.

PAKENHAM, THOMAS. *Meetings with Remarkable Trees.* New York: Random House, 1998. First published in 1996 by Weidenfeld & Nicolson.

———. *Remarkable Trees of the World.* New York: Norton, 2002. First published by Weidenfeld & Nicolson.

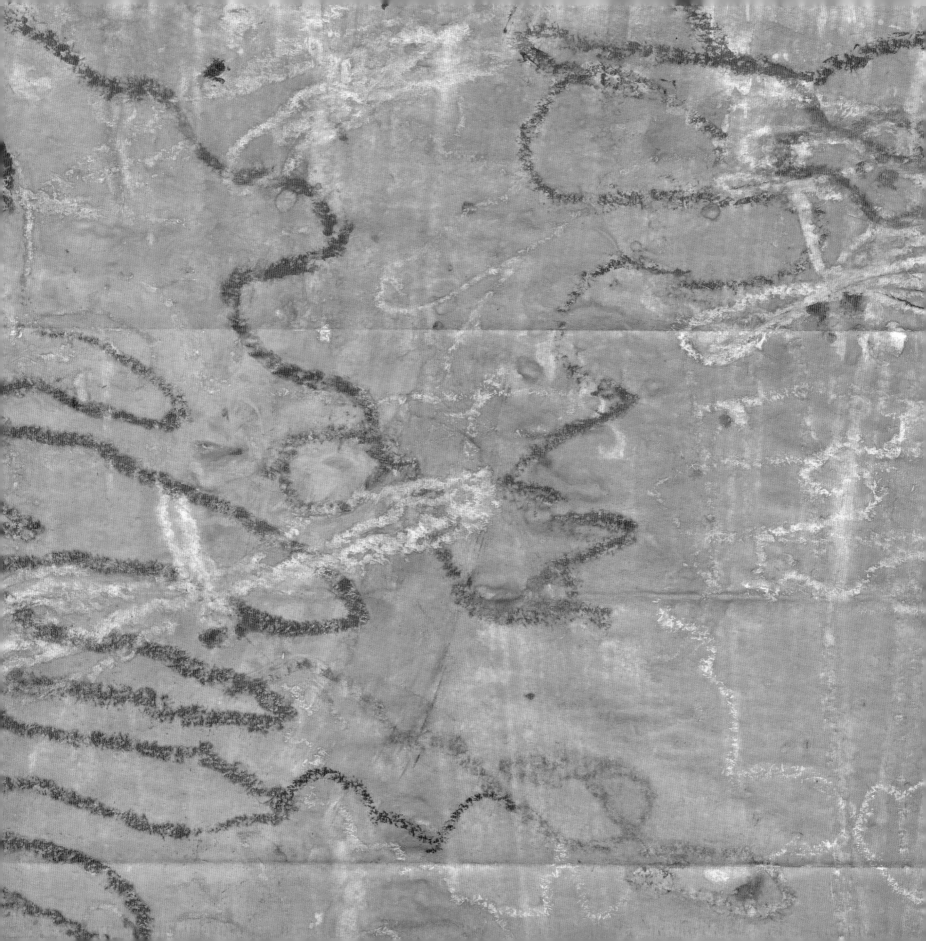